Saraswata's Short Stories

With all the due credits to my teachers, family, parents, friends and companions, who have constantly supported me throughout and let this book possible.

I'd give all the accreditations I receive, to them who have wholeheartedly complemented me in the due course of time, my Mum and my elder sister.

Stardust Serenede

Saraswata's Short Stories, Volume 1

Saraswata Bhattacharya

Published by Saraswata Bhattacharya, 2023.

This is a work of fiction. Similarities to real people, places, or events are entirely coincidental.

STARDUST SERENEDE

First edition. July 1, 2023.

Copyright © 2023 Saraswata Bhattacharya.

Written by Saraswata Bhattacharya.

Also by Saraswata Bhattacharya

Saraswata's Short Stories
Stardust Serenede

Watch for more at https://linktr.ee/Onemanwithamilliondreams.

Dedicated to my parents and eldersister who have supported and complemented me throughout......

Unexpected Twist

David was on a date with Daisy. They were having candle light dinner at one of the finest restaurants of Paris, the renowned city of love.

David held Daisy's hand and produced a diamond ring to her and kissed her hand. In a kneel down position, he proposed to her which she grandly accepted. Next they went for a lip kiss, continuing for a minute or two for a straight, getting duefully romantic and high.

Next when Daisy was asked if she was ready to move into their hotel room, she said something who held David by shock. She received this was just a paid relationship by her boss which was to end that night and that she already had three kids with him.

Illusory Reference

I was a kid when this incident occurred. While travelling back to Kolkata from New Jalpaiguri in 2014, it was already 10:30 at night but we were watching a horror film together. By the time it was 12, we all were off to sleep. The next instant of restless sleeping got really horrendous as my berth was shaking like hell. When I suddenly woke up to a noise, I could see the train had stalled, lights off and a ghostly figure infront of me.

The Man In Disguise

Being a shopkeeper, I was waiting for customers as usual. It was a regular day with light drizzle in the wee hours of July and not much people were there on the road; Henceforth not much customers could be found. A sunglassed man with a blue briefcase in hand suddenly appeared on the scene. He came to my shop and asked for a lighter to lit his cigarette with left hand. He whispered into my ears that cops were behind him, for he was on a robbery spree of some million dollar platinum necklace. I quickly produced to him a packet of biscuits, two packs of gold flake, a pepper spray and rat killer poison as instructed.

When it came to his paying of the money, he quickly tore a pack of gold flake and lit it. His showing of the gold flake drew suspicion, for he actually started chainsmoking, forgetting that he was on the run. When I asked him what's the matter, he was rather fluent in response, but with a pause- I was put on red target at the back of my head with a revolver.

The man was an undercover secret agent in disguise who finally managed to get hold of my years long trade of smuggling of Foreign Liquor and tobacco from Jamaica. I was caught redhanded with an inch of space between me and my destiny.

Surreal Identity

The heavily shirted man with a huge briefcase was moving down fast through the corridor and reached my shop, at a fast pace. It was a rainy day and not many people were out on the streets and I was basically booing away flies from the sweetmeat containers, and eagering idly.

"Umm, a packet of gold flake, the premium quality and two premium quality lighters. Tell me the bill, be quick" said the man in an arrogant manner with the strange heavy briefcase still holding to his left arm.

I quickly produced to him what he wanted, in a black plastic bag sensing something wasn't right. But with a smiling face, I presented myself, hiding my inner curiosity under a blanket of cold smile. "Rs 650 sir, anything else you want?" Said I. "I have quite much of every daily essentials available."

"Don't act smart and give me a two sets of rat killers so that my bill reaches a thousand rupees." He replied blatantly. "Better be quick or I shall......" Before he could complete, I brought his desired stuff in front of them and said, "Here are they, master!"

"Quickly keep this silver chain. I wanted to present it to my wife but I'm short on cash, besides, I've a plane to catch." He said while putting the thin chain on my display rack and rushed away in such kind of hurry which inundated into my curiosity like no other thing could have ever done before, but quickly

Minutes later, two police officers literally ran to my store and enquired of the strange man who had passed by mine just a few minutes later. I got tensed and somewhat managed to say that I recently sold to him cigarettes, lighters and perfumes and got paid in a silver chain. The officers were quick to get hold of the chain and said it was a stolen chain from some of the rarest of antiques of Indian Museum, Kolkata. I was happy and sad at the same time for being able to help in recovering the stolen masterpiece but repented for selling goods to a man without receiving remuneration. Afterall, I wasn't arrested for being a witness or prime suspect and that was all that mattered to me at that moment.

The Phone Call

It was late on Sunday evening when I was just gearing up to finish my sis's portrait by the night's end, when I decided to call upon Daniel for the next day-out's confirmation. I had been pretty reliant on my near-sort-of bestie till date but no longer am I. The call was picked up by an unfamiliar voice of him who was supposedly trying to hide something from me. He purposely lied about his Monday morning maths tuition while also refraining from telling about his advancements' whereabouts citing to poor network and bad stomach. I understood every differential change inside the spam of 5 minutes. I couldn't afford to bear another Steward. My trust broke and our sweet friendship gave over.

Moral:- Trust but blindly. Any crow can be a peacock in disguise, while a foe in friend indeed.

The Fault in our Stars

He held my hand and said while putting his head with silky hair on my lap, "I can only wish, that we could live together forever, but there's a fault in our stars, that destiny won't let us cross our path by any means."

I started sobbing and asked him to shut up. "Darling, what makes you say so, afterall I'm not like other girls who are disloyal or fall for the lust of so-called love making." Said I."I'm here, just for you, always for you and forever for you, by your side and in your heart. Promise me you shall never leave me alone."

He raised his eyes up and looked into the stars. It was a clear night with no clouds and prominent stars made them to their romantic stargazing at midnight. He said slowly, with pauses, while teardrops fell from his eyes, "Fortunes don't match for some reasons we can never interpret; never decipher- for the fault lies in our stars, our fate, sweetheart. I shall always love you from the core of my heart, and that's a promise for sure." He got up from my lap and turned to my face for a lip kiss, and said post, "I'll have to leave for tomorrow, for my fortune lies next to leaving this city tomorrow, leaving you and my sweetheart for a job offer I received abroad. Promise me you'll learn to live alone without me, and for me."

I became shellshocked- literally maintaining a teary and heartbreaking silence for about a minute, both staring at each other's eyes as if future had lost its focus and time stopped flowing way within. I blubbered, nonchalantly in a tone that was subtle, that was wanted not to be told but it was a question of curiosity for me –

"Where, for how long? Will you be alone, my man? Why don't you speak a word? What type of job is it, dear? Man, you got a tongue to speak don't you? What the hell has happened to you.....?"

HE LOST HIS CONSCIOUSNESS and collapsed. I was heartbroken. After reaching his house while carrying him on my back, I discovered that he had haemophilia and was going to die any time soon in the near future. At the same that, he didn't fainted but passed away, for he was breathless- and without a pulse. I was left broken ◈ and our relationship came to a tragic end.

The Blacksmith's Black Magic

Once upon a time in a small village, nestled amidst towering mountains, there lived a skilled blacksmith named Marcus. He was known throughout the land for his remarkable craftsmanship and ability to shape metal with precision. However, the villagers whispered behind closed doors about the source of his uncanny talents. They believed that Marcus possessed a mysterious power, a dark magic that allowed him to forge objects of unparalleled quality.

Marcus, aware of the rumors, paid little attention to them. He knew his skill came from years of dedication and relentless practice, but he did harbor a secret. Hidden deep within the recesses of his workshop was a small black book. This book contained ancient runes and forbidden knowledge—spells and incantations whispered to him by a long-forgotten sorcerer.

One gloomy evening, as the moon cast eerie shadows across the village, a desperate visitor named Alistair arrived at Marcus' door. Alistair was a young man in search of a unique weapon, one that could protect him from the looming danger that threatened his family. With his heart heavy with worry, he pleaded with Marcus to forge a weapon unlike any other.

Intrigued by Alistair's desperation, Marcus agreed to the task. He retreated to his workshop and dusted off the old black book. His fingers traced the ancient symbols, summoning the power that lay dormant within them. As the words rolled off his tongue, the room filled with an otherworldly aura. The blacksmith's hands glowed with an ethereal light as he began shaping the metal, guided by unseen forces.

Weeks passed, and Marcus toiled ceaselessly, pouring his heart and soul into the creation of the weapon. Alistair would often visit, his hope renewed with each glimpse of the blacksmith's progress. Yet, the villagers began to grow wary. The stories of Marcus's magic had spread, and they feared the weapon he was crafting would bring nothing but destruction.

One evening, a gathering of concerned villagers confronted Marcus outside his workshop. Their faces etched with worry and fear, they demanded answers.

Marcus, humbled by their distress, assured them that his intentions were pure. He explained that his gift was not malevolent, but rather a means to channel his artistry and create extraordinary works. Despite his words, doubt lingered in the air.

The following day, Marcus completed the weapon—a magnificent sword forged with impeccable precision. Its blade shimmered with a silvery glow, imbued with an energy that resonated through the very air. With a heavy heart, Marcus presented the weapon to Alistair, who marveled at its beauty.

However, as the villagers observed from a distance, their trepidation reached its peak. Fear blinded their judgment, and they accused Marcus of consorting with dark forces. They surrounded him, their faces twisted with anger and suspicion. Alistair, grasping the sword tightly, stood before Marcus, defending the blacksmith he had come to trust.

In a desperate attempt to prove his innocence, Marcus reached for the black book, determined to show the villagers that his magic was nothing more than a misunderstood gift. He flipped through the pages, searching for a spell to dispel their fears. Yet, in his haste, his hand brushed against a forbidden incantation—the one spell capable of summoning a dark power beyond his control.

Suddenly, a surge of energy enveloped the blacksmith, emanating from the very pages he had touched. The air crackled with electricity as a vortex of darkness formed around Marcus, swallowing him whole. Alistair and the villagers gasped, paralyzed by the sight before them.

When the darkness dissipated, Marcus stood before them, his eyes gleaming with an ancient wisdom. The magic had changed him, transforming him into a mystical creature who could not be uncovered.

The Midnight Romance

In the quaint town of Rosewood, nestled amidst rolling hills and fragrant meadows, there lived a young woman named Lily. Her heart danced to the rhythm of adventure, and her spirit yearned for love's enchantment. Night after night, she found herself gazing at the moon, dreaming of a midnight romance that would whisk her away on a journey of passion and wonder.

One fateful evening, as the clock struck twelve and the moon hung high in the velvety sky, Lily decided to follow the whispers of her heart. She adorned herself in a flowing gown the color of moonlight, her hair cascading in soft waves around her shoulders. With a hint of anticipation in her eyes, she ventured into the moonlit garden, seeking the enchantment she had longed for.

As Lily stepped among the fragrant blooms, a gentle breeze carried with it a sweet melody—a song that seemed to weave its way through the night air. Entranced by its ethereal allure, she followed the sound to a clearing illuminated by moonbeams. There, beneath a towering willow tree, stood a figure bathed in a soft glow.

It was a young man with eyes as deep as the night sky and a smile that captured her heart. He held a violin against his shoulder, his fingers gliding effortlessly across the strings, coaxing a melody that resonated with Lily's very soul. The music enveloped her, wrapping her in a spell of enchantment.

Time stood still as the young man lowered the violin and extended a hand to Lily. With a sparkle in her eyes and a smile that mirrored his, she accepted his invitation, and they danced under the moon's watchful gaze. Their steps were synchronized, their bodies swaying to an invisible rhythm, as if their hearts had known this dance for centuries.

Words were unnecessary between them, for their connection transcended the boundaries of speech. Their laughter blended with the night breeze, their joy echoing through the moonlit garden. As the night deepened, their dance took them through secret paths and hidden corners, exploring a world illuminated by moonlight and shared dreams.

They waltzed through meadows strewn with stardust, twirled on cobblestone streets adorned with fairy lights, and dipped beneath the arches of an ancient bridge, their laughter blending with the gentle trickle of the river below. They were like two celestial beings, entwined in a dance that seemed to bridge the realms of reality and fantasy.

But as the first glimmers of dawn painted the horizon, their dance slowed, and a bittersweet longing settled in their hearts. They knew that the night, with all its magic, was drawing to a close. The young man guided Lily to a stone bench bathed in the soft morning light, and they sat, their hands intertwined, cherishing the final moments of their midnight romance.

With a tender gaze, the young man whispered words that would forever reside in Lily's heart. He spoke of the beauty he had found in her, the way her spirit had ignited his own, and how their meeting beneath the moon's gentle glow had brought a touch of magic into his life. Tears welled in Lily's eyes, for she knew that their time together was fleeting.

As the sun peeked over the horizon, casting golden hues upon the garden, the young man leaned in and kissed Lily's forehead. It was a kiss filled with tenderness and promise—a whispered vow that their midnight romance would forever hold a cherished place in their souls.

And so, as the sky brightened and the world awakened, Lily watched as the young man disappeared into the morning mist, leaving her with a heart overflowing with love and a memory etched in stardust. She returned home, her spirit forever touched by the magic. Her dream of true love had finally come true.

Essence of Maya's Adventure

In the vibrant city of Calcutta, where the streets buzzed with life and colors danced in harmony, there lived a young girl named Maya. With her curious eyes and an insatiable thirst for adventure, she roamed the bustling markets and narrow alleys, her heart yearning for a delightful escapade.

One fine morning, as the sun painted the sky in shades of gold, Maya stumbled upon a weathered map tucked away amidst a stack of old books in a small second-hand bookstore. The map whispered tales of hidden treasures and forgotten secrets, promising an adventure beyond her wildest dreams.

Unable to resist the call of the unknown, Maya clutched the map close to her heart and set off on her grand adventure. With each step, she delved deeper into the heart of Calcutta, guided by the cryptic clues etched upon the map. The city unfolded before her, revealing its hidden wonders and captivating mysteries.

Her first clue led her to a bustling tea stall in the heart of the city. The aroma of freshly brewed tea mingled with the tantalizing scent of spices. Maya approached the kind old tea seller, who smiled knowingly. Handing her a steaming cup of masala chai, he whispered, "Seek the rickshaw wallah who sings with the wind."

Intrigued, Maya followed the hint and soon found herself at the doorstep of a rickshaw stand. There, amidst a sea of colorful rickshaws, stood a man with twinkling eyes and a melodious voice. He serenaded the passersby with songs of love and freedom, his voice carrying the hopes and dreams of Calcutta's bustling streets.

Maya approached the rickshaw wallah and shared her adventure. His eyes sparkled with excitement as he revealed his role in her journey. He handed her a small silver key, whispering, "Unlock the gate guarded by time, where whispers of the past still chime."

With the key in hand, Maya embarked on her next quest. She discovered an ancient garden hidden behind a dilapidated gate, overrun by vines and forgotten by time. As she pushed open the gate, a world of forgotten beauty unfolded before her eyes. Statues bathed in moss, flowers bursting with vibrant colors, and a gentle breeze carrying the whispers of generations past welcomed her.

In the heart of the garden, Maya discovered a crumbling statue of a dancing goddess, her delicate features frozen in time. With trembling hands, she reached out and gently turned the statue, revealing a hidden compartment. Inside, she found an exquisite silk scarf embroidered with tales of ancient glory, a testament to Calcutta's rich heritage.

Embracing the scarf, Maya felt a surge of excitement as she realized her adventure was far from over. The next clue led her to a lively street market, where merchants weaved intricate tales with their wares. A jovial flower seller, adorned with marigold garlands, whispered to her, "Follow the river's song to the bridge of dreams."

Following the rhythm of the river, Maya wandered along its banks until she reached a majestic bridge bathed in golden sunlight. As she stepped onto its worn stones, a sense of serenity enveloped her. The river flowed beneath her, singing tales of hope and resilience. It was a bridge that connected the dreams of the past with the aspirations of the future.

Standing on that bridge, Maya realized that her adventure had transformed her. Calcutta had become a part of her soul, woven into the very fabric of her being. The treasures she sought were not material wealth but the moments of joy, the connections she had forged, and the memories that would forever dance in her heart.

With a contented smile, Maya bid farewell to Calcutta. Her memory of the field visit to the insightful city has truly satiated her spirits.

The Tower of Love

In a quaint village nestled amidst rolling hills and vibrant fields, there stood a magnificent tower, known far and wide as "The Tower of Love." Legends whispered of its magical powers, claiming that anyone who ascended to its highest chamber would be blessed with a love that transcended time and touched the very depths of their soul.

Amongst the villagers, there lived a young woman named Isabella, whose heart was filled with an insatiable longing for a love that would ignite her spirit. She had heard tales of The Tower of Love since she was a child and yearned to experience its enchantment firsthand.

Driven by an irresistible curiosity, Isabella embarked on a journey to discover the truth behind the legends. She followed the winding path that led to the tower, her heart beating with anticipation. As she reached its imposing entrance, she was greeted by an elderly caretaker named Elias, who held the key to unlocking the tower's secrets.

Elias, with a twinkle in his eye, shared stories of the tower's origins and the love stories it had witnessed throughout the ages. He handed Isabella a golden key, worn with time, and offered her a gentle smile. "May your heart find the love it seeks," he said, his voice filled with a wisdom that echoed through the corridors of the tower.

With each step she climbed, Isabella felt a sense of anticipation building within her. The tower's spiral staircase seemed to carry her closer to a destiny she had long yearned for. As she ascended, the air grew warmer, and the scent of roses filled her senses, as if the very walls exhaled love.

Finally, Isabella reached the highest chamber, her heart fluttering with a mixture of hope and trepidation. The room was bathed in a soft, ethereal light, casting a warm glow upon its treasures. In the center stood a beautifully carved stone pedestal, upon which lay an ancient book, its pages yellowed with age.

Isabella approached the book with reverence, her fingers trembling as she opened it to a page filled with handwritten prose. The words spoke of love's enduring power, of the strength it bestowed upon those who dared to embrace it fully. With every line she read, Isabella's heart soared, for she knew she had discovered something truly extraordinary.

As she closed the book, her eyes fell upon a reflection in the windowpane—a figure standing in the doorway. It was a young man named Gabriel, whose eyes mirrored her own longing and whose smile melted her heart. Without a word, they embraced, their souls intertwining in a dance of recognition and belonging.

In that moment, Isabella realized that The Tower of Love held a power far greater than she had ever imagined. It was not the tower itself that bestowed love, but rather the journey it inspired within those who sought it. It was a testament to the strength of their own hearts, their willingness to believe in the extraordinary, and the courage to open themselves to love's transformative embrace.

Isabella and Gabriel's love grew, flourishing like the roses that adorned the tower's walls. Their laughter echoed through the chambers, filling the air with joy. And as the years passed, their love became a beacon of hope for all who visited The Tower of Love, inspiring others to embark on their own quests for true and everlasting love.

And so, The Tower of Love stood as a testament to the power of love itself—a reminder that love is not merely found in enchanted towers or mythical places but resides within the depths of our own hearts, waiting to be discovered and shared with the world.

Emancipation Of Desires

Once upon a time, in a small village nestled amidst rolling hills, there lived a young girl named Aria. She was known for her vibrant spirit and an insatiable thirst for adventure. However, Aria's dreams were confined within the boundaries of her village, where traditions held her aspirations captive.

Aria's heart yearned for emancipation. She yearned to explore the world beyond the hills, to chase her dreams unencumbered. But the village, bound by conservative customs, discouraged such audacity. Aria's desires were considered inappropriate for a young woman.

Undeterred by the limitations imposed on her, Aria sought solace in the natural wonders that surrounded her. She would often retreat to a secret spot by the river, a place where her dreams could flow freely. It was here that she met an old woman, whom the villagers referred to as the Wise Sage.

The Wise Sage was known for her ability to understand the deepest desires of one's heart. Sensing Aria's restless spirit, she took the young girl under her wing. The Wise Sage recognized the importance of nurturing dreams and encouraged Aria to believe in herself.

With the Wise Sage as her guide, Aria embarked on a journey of self-discovery. Together, they delved into forgotten books, discovered hidden talents, and unraveled the mysteries of the world. The Wise Sage taught Aria to embrace her desires, to let them be the compass that guided her path.

Word of Aria's transformation reached the ears of the villagers, who were initially aghast at her newfound liberation. But as time went on, they began to witness the radiant joy that emanated from Aria's spirit. They saw how her emancipation of desires allowed her to contribute positively to the community, inspiring others to break free from their own chains.

Aria's journey wasn't without its challenges. There were moments of doubt and fear, but she pressed forward, knowing that her desires were worth pursuing. Along the way, she met fellow dreamers who shared their stories and reinforced her belief in the power of passion.

As the seasons changed, so did Aria. The once-restricted girl blossomed into a woman who radiated strength and resilience. Her emancipation of desires had transformed her village, infusing it with newfound energy and breaking down the walls of conformity.

Aria's story spread far beyond the village, inspiring people from distant lands to examine their own desires and pursue them fearlessly. The concept of emancipation of desires became a beacon of hope, a reminder that one's dreams should never be stifled.

And so, the tale of Aria and the Wise Sage became legend—a testament to the power of embracing one's desires, of breaking free from the constraints that society imposes. Aria's journey taught the world that true freedom lies not in the absence of desires but in their realization.

And so, in the end, Aria not only achieved her own emancipation but also became a catalyst for the emancipation of desires in others, forever changing the lives of countless individuals who dared to dream.

Circumstuck

"Well, so how much is the price you're gonna offer this pen for" said I, trying to bargain the price of one of the finest fountain pens available in the market."I've already given a discount of Rs 50 on the initial price and charged you accordingly. I don't afford to give you any more discounts."

I thought for a second- a brief pause followed by a cold sweat down my temple and I replied quickly to avoid the shopkeeper to add up to counter my wits, "Isn't that you say the same to each and every customer to ask your extra share of profit? That's a damn dishonest means to loot people of extra money. You should better be honest in your business or divine justice will serve you appropriately."

An awestruck shopkeeper, who by no means fell from the sky, countered my reply as expected, "How dare you call me so? I am honest by every means and have every right to earn my share of profit. After all, I too have a family to feed, you understand?! His tone was rather skeptical at first but he turned to sympathise with his family, so that I fell for it. But neither was I an easy guy to be demeaned, for it wasn't the first time I was bargaining; afterall I had been doing it for years together.

I ahemed back, "You know what? Prices of stuff are increasing because of inflation. Ever heard the word? It's a balloon you know, just gets filled up with as much air as it gets, and bursts at last."

He prayed to God, "Darn it, Holy Heavens! Who am I talking to and even wasting time? Such a second honest person like me, on this wicked Earth? Impossible! I pray to thee that I live free.

"If you are really such honest then who was the man manipulating the price tags of the pens the last day in the evening, huh? You sharply increased the prices by Rs 250 and giving a vague and immodest discount of Rs 50 on it? You can't be lieing now, for you're caught red handed as I've already recorded a video of your wrongdoing." I retorted. "If you don't want me to complain to the company and get your license banned, you better remove that sticker and price me the original value. Or I'll.....".

"I'm very sorry, sir. Just pay me the original price and get away with your stuff. And please don't complain..... I shall not be repeating it......

I got my pen at 90% of the price and got away with it. Afterall it was my years of expertise that helped me escape with a close bargain, without originally having any sort of video!!

Stardust Serenade

Chapter 1: The Celestial Prelude

In the small town of Arcadia, nestled amidst rolling hills and lush green meadows, there lived a young woman named Amelia. She possessed a heart filled with dreams that stretched far beyond the confines of her quiet hometown. Amelia had always felt a deep connection to the stars, finding solace in their twinkling beauty and the mysteries they held.

On a warm summer's night, as Amelia lay on a blanket in a nearby field, she gazed up at the vast expanse of the night sky. Each twinkle of a star seemed to whisper secrets, and a gentle breeze carried the faint melody of an unknown song. Amelia closed her eyes, letting the stardust dance around her, and imagined a world where her dreams could come true.

Chapter 2: Echoes of Destiny

Amelia's reverie was interrupted by the sound of distant music, carried on the wind. She sat up, bewildered, and followed the ethereal melody to its source. It led her to an old, forgotten music box nestled within a cluster of wildflowers. As she touched the weathered surface, the music grew louder and more enchanting.

Spellbound, Amelia listened as the melody swirled around her, filling the night air. In that moment, the stars seemed to align, and she knew that this was a sign from the universe. The music box was a key to her destiny, a catalyst that would transport her on a journey beyond her wildest imagination.

Chapter 3: The Enchanted Voyage

The next morning, Amelia embarked on a quest to unlock the mysteries of the music box. Armed with determination and curiosity, she sought the guidance of an elderly wise woman named Elara, renowned for her knowledge of the arcane. Elara revealed that the music box was imbued with celestial magic, its enchanting melody a pathway to a hidden realm known as Stardust Serenade.

Elara instructed Amelia to gather three celestial artifacts—a moonstone pendant, a comet's tail feather, and a rare starflower—to activate the music box's magic and open the portal to Stardust Serenade. With a map in hand and her heart brimming with hope, Amelia set off on her journey across lands unknown.

Chapter 4: The Moonstone's Glow

Amelia's first destination was the Moonlit Grove, a sacred forest where moonlight bathed the ancient trees in a shimmering glow. She encountered mystical creatures and overcame treacherous obstacles, but her determination never wavered. After a perilous search, she found the moonstone pendant, its luminescent beauty pulsating with celestial energy.

Chapter 5: Following the Comet's Trail

Guided by the whispers of the wind, Amelia embarked on the second leg of her journey to the Celestial Peaks, where a comet's tail feather was said to be hidden. Scaling treacherous cliffs and braving the frigid winds, she finally reached the summit. There, amidst a dazzling display of shooting stars, she discovered the precious feather, its iridescent colors a testament to the wonders of the cosmos.

Chapter 6: A Blossom Among the Stars

Amelia's final destination took her deep into the Nebula Gardens, a place where stars bloomed like flowers in a celestial meadow. It was rumored that a rare starflower, which bloomed only once every century, held the key to unlocking the full power of the music box. With unwavering determination, she traversed the ethereal gardens, guided by the faint glow of the starflower. As she gently plucked the delicate blossom, the air filled with a symphony of celestial harmonies.

Chapter 7: The Stardust Serenade

Armed with the moonstone pendant, the comet 's tail feather, and the rare starflower, Amelia returned to Arcadia. She carefully placed each artifact into the music box, and as the final piece clicked into place, a brilliant burst of stardust erupted from within. A portal opened before her, revealing a breathtaking realm of swirling colors and shimmering constellations.

Stepping through the portal, Amelia found herself in Stardust Serenade—a world where dreams were made manifest and the celestial realms intertwined with reality. The stardust serenade whispered its secrets to her, revealing her true purpose and the power she held within.

Chapter 8: The Cosmic Symphony

In Stardust Serenade, Amelia discovered her calling as a guardian of dreams, tasked with ensuring that the wishes of all souls were heard by the stars. With the music box as her guide, she journeyed across the realms, bringing hope and inspiration to those in need. Each night, her melodies blended with the symphony of the cosmos, harmonizing with the dreams of all who slumbered.

Amelia's tale became legend, and her name echoed through the ages. The stardust serenade resonated in the hearts of those who heard it, reminding them that dreams are the celestial threads that connect us all. And so, Amelia danced under the starlit sky, forever weaving the melodies of the universe and inspiring others to reach for their own stardust serenade.

Epilogue: A Song Never Forgotten

As generations passed, the legend of Amelia and her stardust serenade lived on. The music box, now a cherished relic, remained a symbol of hope and the power of dreams. Its enchanting melody continued to stir the hearts of those who gazed at the night sky, igniting a desire to chase their own dreams and write their own celestial symphony. And so, the tale of Stardust Serenade echoed through time, reminding all who listened that the universe holds infinite possibilities for those who dare to dream.

Cosmos Of Love And Loss

C hapter 1: Celestial Encounters
In the vast expanse of the universe, where stars twinkle like distant dreams, two souls embarked on an extraordinary journey. Sarah, an astronomer with a passion for unraveling the mysteries of the cosmos, had always felt a profound connection to the stars. Lucas, an artist with a soul longing for inspiration, found solace in the beauty of the night sky.

Their paths crossed one summer evening at a stargazing event, where Sarah was giving a talk about the wonders of the universe. Lucas, captivated by her enthusiasm and knowledge, approached her after the event. They engaged in conversations that transcended time and space, igniting a flame that would set their lives on an unforeseen trajectory.

Chapter 2: Dancing Among Nebulas

As their connection grew, Sarah and Lucas spent countless nights beneath the stars, sharing dreams, fears, and aspirations. Amidst their passionate discussions, they discovered a shared longing for adventure and a thirst for the unknown. Together, they decided to embark on a journey to witness the cosmos in all its glory.

With telescopes in hand, they traveled to remote corners of the world, seeking the darkest skies and the clearest views. From the rugged mountains of Chile to the serene plains of Africa, they witnessed celestial wonders beyond imagination—nebulae painting the sky with vibrant hues, galaxies swirling like cosmic ballets, and stars twinkling like distant promises.

Chapter 3: Celestial Embrace

As Sarah and Lucas delved deeper into the mysteries of the universe, they also explored the intricacies of their own hearts. Their love blossomed, becoming as vast and infinite as the cosmos itself. In each other's arms, they found solace, warmth, and inspiration.

But the cosmic dance of love is not without its challenges. Sarah's dedication to her work sometimes consumed her, leaving Lucas feeling lost and neglected.

And as Lucas poured his emotions onto his canvases, he struggled to balance his art with the demands of their journey.

Chapter 4: Shadows in the Starlight

The strains of their individual pursuits began to cast shadows on their once-illuminated path. Sarah, torn between her love for the stars and her love for Lucas, found herself facing an impossible choice. And Lucas, wrestling with his own insecurities, feared that his art would never be enough to capture the essence of their love.

Their journey to the cosmos of love and loss reached a critical juncture. Would they be able to navigate the treacherous tides and find a way to reconcile their passions? Or would the forces of the universe tear them apart, leaving behind only the remnants of a love that once burned bright?

Chapter 5: The Cosmic Reunion

In the midst of their inner turmoil, Sarah and Lucas stumbled upon a cosmic event of rare significance—a supernova, the explosive demise of a massive star. As they witnessed the celestial spectacle, the brilliance of the dying star illuminated their hearts. In that moment, they understood that love, like the stars, can burn brightly but also face its end.

Realizing the fragility of their connection, they made a pact to cherish the time they had together, embracing the beauty of every fleeting moment. Sarah recommitted herself to balancing her love for Lucas and her passion for the stars, while Lucas found inspiration in the impermanence of their love, pouring his emotions onto his canvases like never before.

Epilogue: Love Among the Stars

In the end, Sarah and Lucas discovered that love, just like the universe, is a vast and ever-changing tapestry. Their journey to the cosmos of love and loss taught them to find beauty in both the constancy and transience of life.

Years later, Sarah's groundbreaking research in astrophysics led to new discoveries, revolutionizing our understanding of the cosmos. Lucas, now a renowned artist, captured the essence of their love and the wonders of the universe in his masterpieces.

Their love story, whispered among the stars, became a beacon of hope and inspiration for generations to come. For in the vastness of the universe, amidst the ebb and flow of love and loss, their souls found eternal belonging.

And so, the cosmos of love and loss continues to shine, reminding us that even amidst the grandeur of the stars, the most profound mysteries lie within the human heart.

Elucidating Elements

Chapter 1: The Mysterious Letter

Sarah Taylor was an ordinary woman leading a mundane life. She worked as a librarian in a small town, spending her days surrounded by books. One sunny afternoon, as she sorted through a pile of returned books, an envelope caught her attention. It was addressed to her and bore no return address.

Curiosity piqued, Sarah opened the envelope and found a single sheet of paper inside. The message was cryptic: "Seek the truth within the Elucidating Elements. Your life depends on it."

Confused and intrigued, Sarah couldn't shake off the feeling that something important was at stake. She decided to investigate the meaning of the message, embarking on a thrilling journey.

Chapter 2: The Enigmatic Bookstore

Sarah delved into research about the Elucidating Elements, but her efforts yielded no results. Frustrated, she sought solace in her favorite local bookstore, where she met the eccentric owner, Mr. Simmons. Something about him seemed familiar, as if he held a key to her questions.

Sarah cautiously shared her story with Mr. Simmons, who raised an eyebrow and disappeared into the depths of the bookstore. Moments later, he reappeared with a dusty tome in his hands. The title read "The Elucidating Elements: Unraveling Secrets of the Universe."

Chapter 3: The Hidden Messages

Sarah eagerly flipped through the pages, finding passages filled with cryptic symbols and enigmatic illustrations. It became apparent that the Elucidating Elements were more than just a book. They held secrets beyond her wildest imagination.

As Sarah continued to decipher the hidden messages within the book, she stumbled upon a series of strange symbols. After painstaking research, she discovered they were coordinates leading to a remote location—an abandoned mansion on the outskirts of town.

Chapter 4: The Haunted Mansion

Undeterred by the chilling legends surrounding the mansion, Sarah ventured forth. The sprawling estate was shrouded in mystery and decay, and she could feel the weight of secrets hanging in the air. With each step, the tension mounted.

Inside the mansion, Sarah discovered a hidden chamber concealed behind a bookshelf. There, she found a series of ancient artifacts that seemed to possess a supernatural aura. It became clear that the Elucidating Elements were more than just a book—they were a gateway to a hidden world of knowledge.

Chapter 5: The Secret Society

Sarah's investigation took a dangerous turn when she stumbled upon a clandestine society known as the Guardians of Enlightenment. The society had protected the knowledge contained within the Elucidating Elements for centuries, ensuring it did not fall into the wrong hands.

As Sarah dug deeper into the society's secrets, she discovered a conspiracy of epic proportions. The Guardians had been infiltrated by a renegade faction seeking to exploit the Elucidating Elements' power for their own nefarious purposes.

Chapter 6: The Final Confrontation

Sarah raced against time, desperate to unravel the truth and prevent catastrophe. She sought allies among the remaining loyal members of the Guardians, gathering information that would expose the traitors and restore balance.

In a climactic showdown, Sarah confronted the renegade leader—a former Guardian corrupted by greed and ambition. The battle was intense, with Sarah using her newfound knowledge and determination to overcome the odds.

Chapter 7: The Epilogue

With the traitors defeated and the Elucidating Elements secure, Sarah emerged as a hero. The town hailed her bravery, but she knew her life had been forever changed. The quest for knowledge had led her down a path she never could have imagined, leaving her with more questions than answers.

As Sarah returned to her quiet life as a librarian, she couldn't help but wonder what other mysteries lay hidden within the pages of books

And the world around her. The Elucidating Elements had sparked a hunger for truth that would never be extinguished.

And so, Sarah Taylor's journey continued, her thirst for knowledge and adventure driving her forward into a future filled with endless possibilities.

Demand of Desire

Chapter 1: A Dark Prophecy

In the heartland of India, nestled among the ancient ruins and lush landscapes, a small village named Shaktipur existed in an eerie silence. The villagers whispered tales of a dark prophecy that foretold of a curse that would befall the village. They believed that a relentless desire would consume the souls of its inhabitants, driving them to madness and destruction.

Chapter 2: The Enigmatic Stranger

As the village lived under the ominous shadow of the prophecy, a stranger arrived. His name was Vikram Sharma, a tall and enigmatic man whose piercing blue eyes held a secret knowledge. Rumors spread that he possessed the power to fulfill the deepest desires of anyone who sought his assistance.

Chapter 3: The Desperate Dreamer

Among the villagers was Maya, a young woman consumed by her longing for a life beyond the confines of the village. Driven by an insatiable desire for freedom, Maya sought out Vikram Sharma, hoping he could grant her the means to escape her mundane existence.

Chapter 4: The Sinister Bargain

Vikram Sharma, aware of the prophecy that hung over Shaktipur, had his own agenda. He offered Maya a deal—a pact that would give her the freedom she craved, but at a steep price. Maya, blinded by her desperation, accepted the bargain without fully comprehending its consequences.

Chapter 5: The Spiral of Temptation

As Maya's dreams started to manifest, the village watched in awe and envy. They saw her rise from the ashes of her former life, seemingly untouched by the curse that plagued them all. Her newfound success fueled a vicious cycle of temptation, as others in Shaktipur approached Vikram Sharma with their own desires, oblivious to the darkness that lurked beneath.

Chapter 6: The Mysterious Murders

As the village became consumed by their insatiable desires, a series of mysterious murders plagued Shaktipur. The bodies of those who had made bargains with Vikram Sharma turned up, their faces frozen in expressions of sheer terror. Whispers of a vengeful force seeking justice spread among the villagers, but no one could fathom the true nature of the horror that awaited them.

Chapter 7: Unveiling the Truth

In the midst of chaos, a young investigative journalist named Ravi took interest in the strange happenings of Shaktipur. Determined to uncover the truth behind the murders, he delved deep into the village's past, unearthing a web of dark secrets and suppressed desires.

Chapter 8: The Dance of Deception

As Ravi's investigation progressed, he found himself entangled in a complex dance of deception. Hidden alliances, long-held grudges, and forgotten sins were exposed, each revealing a piece of the puzzle that connected the curse, Vikram Sharma, and the desires that haunted Shaktipur.

Chapter 9: The Final Confrontation

In a race against time, Ravi confronted Vikram Sharma, revealing the extent of his knowledge. The two engaged in a battle of wits and wills, each determined to outmaneuver the other. As the truth unraveled, the curse that had gripped Shaktipur for generations seemed poised to claim its final victims.

Chapter 10: Redemption Or Ruin

In a heart-stopping climax, Ravi discovered the ancient source of the curse—a long-forgotten deity who demanded appeasement for the villagers' uncontrolled desires. With the knowledge he had gathered, Ravi devised a plan to break the cycle of the curse and free Shaktipur from its grip.

As the villagers faced the consequences of their desires, a moral reckoning awaited them. Some found redemption, while others

Met a tragic end. And as the dust settled, Shaktipur would forever be changed, a testament to the price one pays for their deepest desires.

"Demand of Desire" was a tale of mystery, suspense, and vindication—a testament to the power of desire and the darkness that lurks within. In the end, it left a haunting question in the minds of those who read it—what would they be willing to sacrifice to fulfill their own desires?

Shadows of Calcutta

Chapter 1: The Enigmatic Arrival
Calcutta, 1952.

The monsoon rains relentlessly pounded the crowded streets of Calcutta, washing away the sins and secrets that lurked in every corner. Amongst the chaos and poverty, a stranger arrived, shrouded in mystery. His name was Alexander Sinclair, a tall, enigmatic figure with piercing blue eyes and a briefcase that never left his side.

Chapter 2: An Unexpected Encounter

Young journalist, Ravi Sen, found himself drawn to the aura of intrigue surrounding Alexander Sinclair. Ravi had always been captivated by tales of the unexplained, and this stranger seemed to hold the key to a world of secrets. Determined to uncover the truth, Ravi tracked down Sinclair and arranged a clandestine meeting.

Chapter 3: The Hidden Agenda

Over cups of steaming Darjeeling tea in a dimly lit teahouse, Sinclair revealed the purpose of his visit to Calcutta. He claimed to possess information that could unveil a shocking conspiracy involving influential figures in the city. Ravi, driven by his thirst for the truth, offered his assistance in exchange for the exclusive story that could make his career.

Chapter 4: The Mysterious Disappearance

Sinclair and Ravi began their investigation, delving into the dark underbelly of Calcutta's elite. As they got closer to the truth, a chilling twist unfolded. Sinclair vanished without a trace, leaving Ravi bewildered and uncertain. Determined to find his missing ally, Ravi embarked on a perilous journey that would unravel a web of deception and betrayal.

Chapter 5: A Sinister Society

Ravi discovered that Sinclair had been pursuing a secret society known as "The Order of Shadows," a clandestine group rumored to have controlled Calcutta's political and economic landscape for decades. In his pursuit of Sinclair, Ravi encountered a mysterious woman named Maya, who claimed to have ties to the enigmatic society.

Chapter 6: The Labyrinthine City

Maya guided Ravi through the labyrinthine streets of Calcutta, revealing hidden secrets and long-buried truths. As they ventured deeper, Ravi discovered that the Order of Shadows was involved in illegal activities, blackmail, and even murder. Their influence extended far beyond Calcutta, reaching into the highest echelons of power.

Chapter 7: The Revelation

In their search for Sinclair, Ravi and Maya unearthed a shocking revelation—a powerful political figure, thought to be dead, was the mastermind behind the Order of Shadows. This revelation threatened to tear Calcutta apart and expose the true face of corruption that had plagued the city for decades.

Chapter 8: A Race Against Time

With the truth at their fingertips, Ravi and Maya found themselves pursued by relentless assassins, determined to silence them before the world learned of the Order's existence. Fleeing from one hiding place to another, they raced against time to bring the evidence to light and expose the true culprits behind the city's dark secrets.

Chapter 9: The Final Showdown

As Ravi and Maya closed in on the truth, they realized that their battle was not only against the Order of Shadows but against the very heart of darkness that enveloped Calcutta. In a final, climactic confrontation, they confronted the mastermind behind the Order and fought to bring justice to a city plagued by corruption and manipulation.

Chapter 10: Shadows Dissipated

In the aftermath of the final showdown, Calcutta stood on the precipice of change. The exposure of the Order of Shadows sent shockwaves through the city's power structures, leading to a reckoning that would shape the future. Ravi,

Having unraveled the mystery that had consumed him, emerged as a beacon of truth in a world that had long been shrouded in shadows.

Epilogue: The Legacy

Years later, the legacy of Ravi's investigation continued to shape Calcutta. The Order of Shadows was dismantled, and the city slowly rebuilt itself, free from the clutches of corruption. Ravi, now an acclaimed journalist, continued to expose hidden truths, ensuring that the shadows would never return to Calcutta.

The End.

Air Fare

Once upon a time in the bustling city of Kolkata, there lived a man named Arjun Mukherjee. Arjun was a middle-aged bachelor who worked as a clerk in a government office. He led a simple and predictable life, with his days filled with paperwork and his evenings spent sipping tea at a local tea stall. But little did Arjun know that his life was about to take a comical turn.

One fine day, as Arjun was going about his usual routine, he stumbled upon a newspaper advertisement for a special discounted airfare to Darjeeling. The ad claimed it was a once-in-a-lifetime opportunity, and Arjun's curiosity was piqued. He had never been on an airplane before, and the idea of traveling to the picturesque hill station excited him.

Without giving it a second thought, Arjun immediately rushed to the travel agency mentioned in the advertisement. As he entered the agency, he was greeted by a young and cheerful air hostess named Riya. She had a pleasant smile and a twinkle in her eyes that caught Arjun's attention.

Arjun, still catching his breath from his rush to the agency, approached the counter where Riya stood.

Arjun: (panting) Excuse me, Miss. I saw the advertisement in the newspaper about the discounted airfare to Darjeeling. Is it still available?

Riya: (smiling) Yes, sir! We still have a few seats left. Darjeeling is a beautiful place to visit, especially during this time of the year. Are you interested in booking a ticket?

Arjun: (excitedly) Absolutely! How much does it cost?

Riya: (checks her computer) The discounted fare is only Rs. 3000 for a round trip, sir.

Arjun: (astonished) Wow, that's unbelievable! Please book a ticket for me right away.

Riya: (typing on the computer) Sure, sir. Could I please have your name?

Arjun: Arjun Mukherjee.

Riya: (still typing) Mr. Arjun Mukherjee, is it? That's a lovely name, sir.

Arjun blushed slightly, flattered by Riya's compliment.

Riya: (continuing) Now, Mr. Mukherjee, can I have your age and contact details, please?

Arjun: (pauses for a moment, thinking) Well, I'm 40 years old, and my contact number is...

Just as Arjun was about to give his phone number, he was interrupted by a loud noise from outside the agency. They both turned towards the source of the commotion and saw a street procession passing by, with people dancing and singing.

Riya: (chuckles) Seems like Kolkata is always full of surprises.

Arjun: (smiling) Indeed. Now, where were we?

Riya: (giggling) Your contact details, sir.

Arjun: (reciting his phone number) It's 9876543210.

Riya: (typing) Perfect. And do you have any specific dates in mind for your trip?

Arjun: (thinking) Hmm, how about next week? I've got a few days off from work, so it would be a good time to go.

Riya: (nodding) Great! I'll book your ticket for next week, starting on Monday. Is that alright?

Arjun: (excitedly) Absolutely! I can't wait to fly for the first time!

Riya: (smiling) I'm sure you'll have a wonderful experience, Mr. Mukherjee. Is there anything else I can assist you with?

Arjun: (pausing for a moment) Actually

, there is one more thing. I've never been on an airplane before, so I'm a bit nervous. Can you give me some tips or information?

Riya: (grinning) Of course, I can! First, please arrive at the airport at least two hours before your flight. It's essential to go through security checks and complete the boarding process.

Arjun: (listening attentively) Alright, two hours before the flight. Got it.

Riya: (continuing) Secondly, make sure you don't carry any prohibited items like sharp objects or liquids exceeding the allowed limit in your hand luggage.

Arjun: (nodding) I'll keep that in mind. No knives or big bottles of water.

Riya: (smiling) Yes, exactly. And during the flight, please fasten your seatbelt when the seatbelt sign is on and keep your mobile phones on flight mode.

Arjun: (smiling nervously) Flight mode, right.

Riya: (encouragingly) Don't worry, Mr. Mukherjee. The cabin crew will provide all the necessary instructions during the flight. Just relax and enjoy the experience.

Arjun: (grinning) Thank you, Miss Riya. You've been really helpful.

Riya: (blushing) You're welcome, Mr. Mukherjee. It's my pleasure to assist you. Have a fantastic trip to Darjeeling!

Arjun bid farewell to Riya and left the travel agency, his heart filled with excitement and anticipation. For the next few days, he couldn't stop thinking about his upcoming flight. He even bought a guidebook on Darjeeling to familiarize himself with the tourist spots.

Finally, the day of the flight arrived. Arjun woke up early, packed his bags, and headed to the airport. As he entered the bustling terminal, he felt a mix of nervousness and exhilaration. He followed Riya's advice and arrived two hours before the scheduled departure.

As Arjun made his way through security and reached the boarding gate, he couldn't help but notice the diverse group of passengers waiting alongside him. There were families with excited children, young couples, and even a group of elderly friends who were traveling together.

Arjun took a deep breath and settled into his seat, fastening his seatbelt as instructed. Moments later, the cabin crew made their way through the aisle, ensuring that everyone was ready for takeoff. Arjun's heart raced as he felt the plane taxiing on the runway, preparing for the magical moment of soaring into the sky.

Just as the plane lifted off, Arjun's nerves began to settle, replaced by a childlike wonder. He peered out of the window and marveled at the sight of Kolkata getting smaller and smaller below him. The city transformed into a colorful mosaic, its streets, and buildings blending into one another.

As the flight progressed, Arjun started feeling hungry. He remembered that a meal was included in the airfare. A flight attendant approached him, holding a tray with a warm meal.

Flight Attendant: (smiling) Good afternoon, sir. Here's your meal. Enjoy!

Arjun: (grinning) Thank you!

Arjun unwrapped the plastic cover from the tray, and to his surprise, he found a small container with a label that read "Kolkata Biryani." His eyes widened in disbelief.

Arjun: (muttering to himself) Kolkata Biryani at 30,000 feet? Now, that's something!

He took a spoonful of the biryani, and the flavors exploded in his mouth. It was a delightful blend of aromatic spices and tender meat, just like the biryanis he had enjoyed back in Kolkata. Arjun couldn

't help but chuckle at the irony of enjoying a taste of Kolkata while soaring high above it.

As the flight continued, Arjun struck up conversations with his fellow passengers, sharing stories and laughter. He realized that air travel had a unique way of bringing people together, transcending their differences and creating a sense of camaraderie.

Finally, the plane began its descent, and Arjun could see the rolling hills of Darjeeling coming into view. The sight took his breath away. The lush green tea gardens, the toy train chugging along the tracks, and the snow-capped peaks of the Himalayas in the distance—it was a sight that surpassed his expectations.

As Arjun stepped out of the aircraft, he couldn't wipe the smile off his face. His first flight had been an unforgettable experience—one filled with excitement, laughter, and a taste of home at 30,000 feet. He thanked the air hostess, Riya, in his mind for making it all possible.

Arjun spent the next few days exploring Darjeeling, savoring the breathtaking views and indulging in the local delicacies. Every moment was etched in his memory, creating a treasure trove of stories to share when he returned to Kolkata.

When the time came to head back home, Arjun felt a pang of sadness. He had fallen in love with Darjeeling, but he knew that he had to return to his everyday life in Kolkata. As the plane took off, he gazed out of the window, bidding farewell to the picturesque hill station.

As the flight glided through the sky, Arjun reflected on his journey. He realized that life was full of unexpected surprises, and sometimes, taking a leap of faith could lead to the most extraordinary experiences. He made a silent promise to himself that he would continue exploring, discovering, and embracing the wonders that life had to offer.

And so, with a heart full of gratitude and memories to cherish, Arjun returned to Kolkata, ready to embark on his next adventure.

The End

Love in the Long Run

Chapter 1: The Fateful Encounter

Calcutta, 1923. The city of joy bustled with life, vibrant colors, and secrets hidden within its narrow lanes. It was a time when tradition clashed with the winds of change, and mystical tales whispered through the humid air.

In the heart of this enchanting city, lived a young woman named Anaya. She possessed a beauty that captured the gaze of many, but her heart remained untouched. Anaya had inherited a fascination for the mystical from her grandmother, who had regaled her with tales of love, destiny, and the hidden powers that governed their lives.

One fateful evening, Anaya found herself wandering through the crowded marketplace. As she navigated through the maze of vendors, a stranger caught her eye. His name was Ravi, a charismatic and mysterious man with deep, penetrating eyes that seemed to hold a thousand stories.

Their eyes met, and in that instant, time stood still. Anaya's heart skipped a beat as if it recognized something long lost. Ravi, too, felt a magnetic pull towards her, an inexplicable connection that defied logic.

Chapter 2: The Unveiling Secrets

Days turned into weeks, and Anaya and Ravi began to spend more time together. In the twilight hours, they would wander through the ancient temples and hidden alleyways of Calcutta, their souls entwined in a dance of shared secrets and unspoken desires.

One evening, as they sought refuge from the chaos of the city, they stumbled upon an old bookstore tucked away in a forgotten corner. Its owner, a wise old man named Pandit Gupta, sensed their extraordinary bond and invited them to explore the mystical realm of ancient scriptures and forgotten texts.

In the depths of the bookstore, Anaya and Ravi discovered a weathered journal that spoke of a powerful talisman said to grant eternal love. Its whereabouts were unknown, lost to time and scattered whispers. Intrigued by the journal's promises, Anaya and Ravi embarked on a quest to uncover the truth behind the legend.

Chapter 3: The Quest for Eternal Love

Their search led them to the hidden enclaves of Calcutta, where they encountered wise sages and mystics who shared cryptic clues and ancient rituals. They followed the trail through dimly lit temples, sacred riverbanks, and opulent palaces.

As Anaya and Ravi delved deeper into their quest, they found themselves entangled in a web of mystery and danger. Dark forces lurked in the shadows, determined to seize the power of the talisman for themselves. Anaya and Ravi's love became their greatest strength, their unwavering bond guiding them through the treacherous path.

Chapter 4: The Final Confrontation

The climax of their journey arrived when they discovered the secret location of the talisman—a mystical cave hidden in the heart of a remote forest. But their arrival triggered a confrontation with the enigmatic cult of the Black Lotus, sworn protectors of the talisman's power.

In a battle of wills, Anaya and Ravi fought side by side against the formidable cult, drawing upon their love and unwavering belief in destiny. With each strike and parry, their determination grew, fueled by the knowledge that their love transcended the boundaries of time.

Chapter 5: Love's Triumph

In the end, love conquered all. Anaya and Ravi emerged victorious, securing the talisman's power and safeguarding it from those who sought to abuse its magic. They returned to Calcutta, their hearts filled with gratitude and an unbreakable bond.

The city celebrated their triumph, their love becoming a symbol of hope and enduring passion. Anaya

And Ravi knew that their journey had not only brought them closer to each other but had also uncovered the true essence of love—a force that transcended time, defied logic, and conquered all obstacles.

In the years that followed, Anaya and Ravi continued to live in Calcutta, their love growing stronger with each passing day. They became pillars of their community, sharing their wisdom and experiences with those in need. Their tale became a legend, passed down through generations, inspiring countless hearts to believe in the power of love.

As the sun set over the enchanting city of Calcutta, Anaya and Ravi stood hand in hand, their eyes reflecting the eternal flame of their love. They knew that their journey had been more than just a quest for a mystical talisman—it had been a journey of self-discovery, of unraveling the mysteries of their own souls.

And as the stars twinkled above, casting their mystical glow upon the city, Anaya and Ravi embraced the magic of their love, knowing that together, they would traverse the long run of life, their hearts forever entwined in a timeless dance of romance and destiny.

Love's Eclipse

Chapter 1: A Chance Encounter

The bustling city of Mumbai, known for its vibrant energy and diverse culture, was a melting pot of dreams and aspirations. Amidst the chaos, destiny often played its cards, bringing together two souls on a path they never anticipated.

Riya, a talented young architect, had recently returned to Mumbai after completing her studies abroad. Her heart brimmed with excitement as she embarked on a new chapter of her life. She was eager to prove herself in the demanding world of architecture.

One sunny afternoon, Riya found herself at a quaint café in Bandra, sipping on her cappuccino and sketching designs in her notebook. As she focused on her work, her attention was momentarily diverted by a captivating melody drifting from across the room. Intrigued, she glanced up and her eyes locked with those of Arjun, a talented musician.

Arjun was engrossed in his guitar, strumming the strings with effortless passion. His music seemed to speak to Riya's soul, creating an instant connection. She found herself lost in the enchanting melodies, oblivious to the world around her. It was as if fate had orchestrated this encounter, drawing them together like a magnetic force.

After Arjun finished his performance, he looked up to find Riya's gaze fixed upon him. He flashed her a warm smile that sent shivers down her spine. Gathering her courage, Riya walked over to him, her heart pounding in her chest.

"Your music is beautiful," she said, her voice filled with genuine admiration.

Arjun's eyes sparkled with gratitude. "Thank you. It means a lot coming from someone as talented as you," he replied, gesturing toward her notebook filled with architectural designs.

They spent the rest of the afternoon engrossed in conversation, sharing their dreams and aspirations. Their passions resonated deeply with each other, igniting a profound connection. It was as if they had known each other for a lifetime.

Chapter 2: Unveiling Shadows

As days turned into weeks, Arjun and Riya's bond grew stronger. They explored the vibrant streets of Mumbai together, finding solace in each other's company. Riya's creative mind blossomed under Arjun's encouragement, while Arjun found inspiration in Riya's unwavering determination.

One evening, as they sat on the beach watching the sun dip below the horizon, Riya confessed her deepest fear. "Arjun, I'm afraid that my dreams might consume me. I'm afraid I won't have time for love."

Arjun gently cupped her face, his eyes filled with tenderness. "Love should never be sacrificed for dreams, Riya. It should fuel them. Together, we can conquer any obstacles that come our way."

Moved by his words, Riya's heart filled with hope. She realized that true love could exist alongside her ambition, enriching her life rather than hindering it.

Chapter 3: Love's Melody

Arjun and Riya's love story unfolded like a symphony, with every note weaving a tale of devotion and passion. Their careers flourished, and their love provided a sanctuary amidst the chaos of their demanding lives.

But like any masterpiece, their journey was not without its share of challenges. Riya's career often took her away from Mumbai, forcing them into long-distance relationship hurdles. Yet, their love remained steadfast, bridging the gap with late-night calls, heartfelt messages, and occasional surprise visits.

Chapter 4: A Lunar Eclipse

One evening, as the city prepared for a rare lunar eclipse, Riya and Arjun found themselves standing on the rooftop of their apartment building, gazing at the night sky. The moon slowly vanished behind a shadow,

Its ethereal glow dimming. The atmosphere was charged with anticipation, mirroring the emotions that enveloped the couple.

Riya leaned against Arjun's shoulder, her hand intertwined with his. "Isn't it mesmerizing how the moon and the sun, two celestial bodies, can create such a beautiful phenomenon together?"

Arjun pressed a tender kiss on her forehead. "Just like us, Riya. We may be two individuals, but when we come together, we create something extraordinary."

As the eclipse reached its peak, Riya couldn't help but feel a sense of unity with the universe. It was a reminder that even in the darkest moments, there was always a glimmer of light waiting to emerge.

Chapter 5: Dancing Shadows

Time flew by, and Arjun and Riya's love deepened with every passing day. They reveled in the simple joys of life, dancing under the rain, stealing kisses in crowded cafes, and embracing the beauty of everyday moments.

One evening, Arjun surprised Riya with tickets to a prestigious music festival where he was scheduled to perform. As the crowd erupted in applause, Riya watched with pride as Arjun commanded the stage, his passion resonating through his music. In that moment, she realized how fortunate she was to be part of his journey.

But amidst the celebration, an unexpected twist of fate awaited them. Riya received an offer for an architectural project in a different city, one that would catapult her career to new heights. It was an opportunity she couldn't ignore, yet it meant leaving behind the life she had built with Arjun.

Chapter 6: Eclipse of the Heart

Riya sat in her empty apartment, surrounded by moving boxes and memories. Her heart ached with the weight of her decision. She had always believed that love and ambition could coexist, but now she found herself at a crossroads, torn between two equally compelling paths.

Days turned into weeks, and the distance between Arjun and Riya seemed insurmountable. The late-night calls grew shorter, and the messages became infrequent. Both hearts yearned for each other, yet circumstances threatened to eclipse their love.

Chapter 7: Rekindling the Flame

With the weight of regret heavy on her shoulders, Riya made a life-altering decision. She couldn't let go of the love she had found in Arjun, nor could she deny her dreams. With determination in her eyes, she boarded a flight back to Mumbai, ready to face whatever awaited her.

Arjun, caught between hope and despair, received the news of Riya's return with equal parts excitement and trepidation. He couldn't deny the emptiness that had consumed him during their time apart, and he prayed that this reunion would rekindle their love.

Chapter 8: A Love Reborn

As Riya stepped off the plane, her heart raced with anticipation. She rushed through the airport, her eyes scanning the crowd until they locked with Arjun's.

The world seemed to fade away as they embraced, their love bridging the distance and washing away the pain of separation.

"I couldn't bear to be without you," Riya whispered, tears of joy streaming down her cheeks.

Arjun kissed her gently, his voice filled with unwavering devotion. "We've weathered the storm, Riya. Our love is stronger than ever."

Together, they embarked on a new chapter, weaving their dreams into a shared future. They learned to embrace the ebb and flow of their careers, knowing that their love would always be their anchor.

Chapter 9: Celestial Harmony

Years passed, and Arjun and Riya's love continued to flourish. They celebrated each other's achievements, lifted each other during moments of doubt, and navigated the

Complexities of life hand in hand. Their individual paths merged seamlessly, creating a symphony of love and harmony.

Riya's architectural projects garnered international acclaim, while Arjun's music touched the hearts of millions. Their love story became a source of inspiration for others, a testament to the power of love and the pursuit of dreams.

Chapter 10: Forever's Eclipse

On a warm summer evening, as the sun began its descent, Arjun and Riya found themselves once again on the rooftop of their Mumbai apartment building. They stood in each other's arms, reminiscing about their journey, and marveling at the eclipses they had weathered together.

"Do you remember that day we first met?" Riya asked, a smile dancing on her lips.

Arjun chuckled softly, his eyes filled with love. "How could I forget? It was the day our hearts aligned."

As darkness settled and the stars began to twinkle in the night sky, Arjun reached into his pocket, revealing a small velvet box. Riya gasped, her hands covering her mouth in surprise.

"Riya, you are the light that has illuminated my world," Arjun began, his voice trembling with emotion. "Will you join me on this journey of love and dreams forever?"

Tears of joy streamed down Riya's face as she nodded, unable to find her voice. Arjun slipped the ring on her finger, sealing their love in an unbreakable bond.

In that moment, under the celestial tapestry of a starlit sky, Arjun and Riya vowed to keep their love burning bright, never allowing it to be eclipsed by the challenges that lay ahead.

Their hearts, once eclipsed by doubt and uncertainty, had found their eternal rhythm—a melody of love, dreams, and a profound understanding that true love and ambition could thrive together.

And so, in the heart of contemporary Mumbai, two souls, forever entwined, embarked on a journey that would forever be remembered as the tale of their eclipsed hearts.

The Veil of Vengeance

Chapter 1: Shadows of Ambition

Detective Michael Pierce sat alone in his dimly lit office, his eyes fixated on the framed photograph of his deceased wife, Sarah. The loss of his beloved had ignited a fire within him—a desire for power and vengeance. Michael had climbed the ranks of the police force, but it was not enough. He craved something more, something that would make the world tremble at his feet.

Chapter 2: The Whispering Dark

Whispers echoed through the corridors of power, rumors of a relentless officer with a vindictive attitude who yearned for the presidency. Michael's aspirations had grown insatiable, and he would stop at nothing to achieve his ultimate goal. The next step on his path to power was eliminating his greatest obstacle: the esteemed Lawrence Mitchell, the Law of Attorney of the Supreme Court.

Chapter 3: Unmasking Shadows

Lawrence Mitchell was a highly respected and influential figure, a symbol of justice and integrity. He had dedicated his life to upholding the law and ensuring justice prevailed. But Michael knew that behind the façade of righteousness, darkness lurked. He delved into Lawrence's past, digging up buried secrets, connections, and vulnerabilities that could be exploited.

Chapter 4: The Mysterious Encounter

On a cold autumn evening, a stranger appeared at Michael's doorstep. The man introduced himself as Victor Grayson, a master manipulator with an extensive network of informants. He offered his services, promising to uncover the darkest secrets of Lawrence Mitchell's life. Intrigued and wary, Michael accepted the enigmatic man's help, knowing that he was dancing with danger.

Chapter 5: The Tangled Web

As Victor Grayson delved into Lawrence Mitchell's past, he discovered a web of deceit, scandal, and corruption. Secrets involving powerful individuals and their hidden agendas began to unravel. Michael's obsession with power was matched only by his thirst for revenge. He realized that by toppling Lawrence, he could expose the rot within the system and claim his rightful place at the helm.

Chapter 6: Dark Alliances

Michael and Victor forged an unholy alliance, weaving a tapestry of deception and manipulation. They enlisted the aid of individuals who shared a similar desire for vengeance against Lawrence Mitchell. These alliances were shrouded in secrecy, with each member contributing their unique skills to the cause. The web tightened, and the forces of darkness prepared to strike.

Chapter 7: A Symphony of Shadows

As the days turned into weeks, the group meticulously orchestrated their plan. They infiltrated Lawrence Mitchell's inner circle, planting seeds of doubt and suspicion. The once-untouchable attorney found himself isolated, his allies falling away like leaves in the wind. Michael reveled in the chaos he had created, his every move calculating and precise.

Chapter 8: The Dance of Death

The night of the grand ball arrived, where the crème de la crème of society gathered. It was the perfect opportunity for Michael to execute his plan. Dressed in a tailored suit, he concealed a deadly weapon, ready to strike when the moment presented itself. As the clock struck midnight, Michael's eyes locked with Lawrence's across the crowded room, and a sinister smile crept across his face.

Chapter 9: The Shattered Illusion

In a moment of brilliance and ruthlessness, Michael unleashed his fury. Chaos erupted as screams filled the air, and blood stained the pristine ballroom floor. The once-mighty Lawrence Mitchell fell, gasping for breath, the light of life fading from his eyes. Michael had exacted his revenge, but at what cost? The consequences of his actions began to unravel, threatening to consume him.

Chapter 10: The Reckoning

As news of Lawrence Mitchell's murder spread like wildfire, shockwaves reverberated through the nation. The loss of such a prominent figure sent ripples of fear and uncertainty across the country. The Supreme Court mourned the loss of one of their own, while the public demanded answers.

Michael had believed that by eliminating Lawrence, he would expose the corruption within the system and propel himself towards the presidency. However, the aftermath of his actions was far more treacherous than he had anticipated.

The investigative spotlight turned toward him, and he found himself entangled in a web of suspicion and deceit.

Chapter 11: A Fractured Mask

The facade of righteousness that Michael had carefully crafted began to crack under the weight of his deeds. As the evidence piled up against him, his vindictive attitude only served to strengthen the case. The public turned against him, viewing him as a monster in uniform. Michael's dream of becoming the President of the United States seemed to fade into oblivion.

Chapter 12: Shadows of Betrayal

In the darkest hour of his life, Michael discovered that Victor Grayson, the enigmatic ally who had aided him in his quest for power, had betrayed him. Victor had been playing a double game all along, using Michael's ambitions to further his own sinister agenda. He had orchestrated Lawrence Mitchell's murder to eliminate a potential threat and frame Michael for the crime.

Chapter 13: The Descent

Michael found himself trapped in a labyrinth of lies, struggling to find a way out. With the weight of guilt and betrayal crushing him, he embarked on a desperate journey to clear his name and unearth the truth. The lines between hunter and hunted blurred as he sought to expose Victor's treachery and bring him to justice.

Chapter 14: The Rabbit Hole

Every step Michael took deeper into the investigation led him down a rabbit hole of secrets and conspiracies. He discovered that Lawrence Mitchell was not the paragon of virtue he had believed him to be. The attorney had been entangled in a web of blackmail, bribery, and illicit dealings, making enemies in high places. The truth became a twisted kaleidoscope of shadows and half-truths.

Chapter 15: Redemption or Ruin

As Michael unraveled the truth, he found himself at a crossroads. Should he seek redemption by exposing the corruption and sacrificing his own ambitions? Or should he succumb to the darkness that had consumed him, embracing the power he had so desperately craved? The choices he made would determine his fate and the future of the nation.

Chapter 16: The Final Confrontation

In a climactic showdown, Michael confronted Victor Grayson, the puppet master behind it all. The two adversaries locked horns, each driven by their own twisted desires. It was a battle of wills, a clash between the forces of vengeance and manipulation. As the truth unfolded, Michael made his stand, fighting not only for his own redemption but for the soul of a nation.

Chapter 17: Shadows of the Past

In the end, justice prevailed. Michael's revelations shook the foundations of power, exposing the corrupt underbelly of the system. The truth had a price, and Michael paid it willingly. He was stripped of his badge and faced the consequences of his actions, but he had sparked a movement—a movement that sought to rebuild a broken system and restore faith in justice.

Epilogue: The Veil Lifted

Years passed, and Michael became a symbol of both hope and caution. His story served as a reminder of the dangers of unchecked ambition and the destructive nature of revenge. The nation rebuilt itself, learning from its past mistakes. The shadows that had once haunted Michael now dissipated, leaving behind a legacy of tragedy and redemption.

And as the years rolled on, a new generation emerged, one that learned from the mistakes of the past. The memory of Michael Pierce, the once-vindictive police officer, became a cautionary tale, a reminder of the dangers of unchecked ambition and the cost of vengeance.

The presidency, once Michael's ultimate goal, was redefined. The country yearned for leaders who embodied integrity, compassion, and a genuine desire to serve the people. The stain of corruption was slowly cleansed, as the nation moved forward with renewed hope.

Lawrence Mitchell's murder remained a tragic chapter in history, a scar that could never fully heal. The Supreme Court honored his memory by continuing to champion justice and uphold the law, forever mindful of the darkness that can lurk within the corridors of power.

In the end, the story of Michael Pierce served as a reminder that the pursuit of power at any cost could only lead to destruction. The shadows of his past haunted him until his last breath, but his downfall sparked a movement, a collective determination to ensure that those who sought high office did so with pure intentions.

And so, the United States trudged forward, forever changed by the tale of a man whose ambitions tore him apart. The veil of vengeance had been lifted, and a new era of governance began—one built on transparency, empathy, and the collective responsibility to never forget the tragic consequences of one man's thirst for power.

Viral Vendetta

Chapter 1: A Scientist's Revelation

Dr. Victor Adams, an eccentric scientist known for his groundbreaking inventions, had been working diligently in his secluded laboratory for years. His latest creation, a revolutionary artificial virus, had the potential to change the world as we knew it. With a heavy heart, he realized that his invention could also become a dangerous weapon if it fell into the wrong hands.

Chapter 2: Unseen Threats

Unbeknownst to Dr. Adams, a notorious terrorist organization called the New Dawn had been monitoring his activities for months. Led by the enigmatic and merciless leader, Omar Al-Rashid, the New Dawn sought to gain power and control by harnessing the destructive capabilities of Dr. Adams' artificial virus.

Chapter 3: The Perfect Storm

The New Dawn's network of spies infiltrated Dr. Adams' laboratory, stealing the virus and leaving a trail of destruction in their wake. The Western intelligence agencies were alerted, realizing the imminent danger that awaited the world. They swiftly formed a joint alliance, pooling their resources to prevent the virus from falling into the wrong hands.

Chapter 4: Pursuit and Betrayal

Agent Emily Thompson, a skilled operative from the CIA, was assigned the task of tracking down the stolen virus. As she delved deeper into the investigation, she discovered a shocking truth—there was a mole within their alliance. Someone high-ranking in one of the Western economies was secretly working for the New Dawn, seeking to sow chaos and destruction.

Chapter 5: Deadly Chase

Agent Thompson embarked on a perilous journey, traversing countries and encountering ruthless assassins sent by the New Dawn. With each step, the tension grew as the world teetered on the brink of annihilation. Time was running out, and the stakes had never been higher.

Chapter 6: The Unveiling

While Agent Thompson closed in on the mole's identity, the New Dawn made a bold move. They unleashed a small sample of the artificial virus, causing panic and chaos in a major city. The world watched in horror as the devastating effects of the virus became apparent—its ability to spread rapidly and wipe out entire populations.

Chapter 7: A Desperate Race

With the clock ticking, Agent Thompson joined forces with Agent James Collins from MI6 and Agent Hiroshi Nakamura from the Japanese intelligence agency. Together, they followed a trail of clues that led them to Iran, where the New Dawn's secret headquarters were located. They had to act swiftly, before the organization released the full force of the virus upon the world.

Chapter 8: A Deadly Confrontation

Infiltrating the New Dawn's stronghold, the agents faced a web of traps and challenges, designed to protect the organization's most valuable asset—the artificial virus. As they fought their way through, the agents were haunted by the knowledge that any misstep could unleash catastrophe on an unimaginable scale.

Chapter 9: Redemption and Sacrifice

In a climactic showdown, Agent Thompson confronted Omar Al-Rashid, the mastermind behind the New Dawn. Their battle was intense, each fighting for their own vision of the world's future. As they clashed, the truth about the mole within the alliance was revealed—a shocking betrayal that threatened to undermine everything they had fought for.

Chapter 10: The Final Stand

With the world on the brink of destruction, the joint alliance of Western economies rallied together. United by their determination to protect humanity, they launched a full-scale assault on the New Dawn's headquarters. In a heart-pounding battle, they fought for their lives and the fate of the world.

Chapter 11: Triumph and Reflection

As the dust settled, the New Dawn was defeated, and the stolen artificial virus was secured. The alliance

Breathed a collective sigh of relief, knowing they had averted a global catastrophe. However, the victory came at a great cost. Many lives were lost, and the scars of the ordeal would forever remain.

In the aftermath, Dr. Adams, wracked with guilt for his unwitting role in the crisis, dedicated his life to developing antidotes and cures for the diseases that plagued humanity. He vowed never again to let his inventions fall into the wrong hands.

Agent Thompson, Agent Collins, and Agent Nakamura received commendations for their bravery and resourcefulness. They were hailed as heroes, but the weight of their experiences weighed heavily on their souls. They knew the darkness that lurked beneath the surface, the fragility of the world they fought to protect.

The joint alliance of Western economies forged stronger ties, recognizing the need for ongoing cooperation in the face of global threats. They implemented stricter security measures and improved intelligence sharing to prevent such a catastrophe from happening again.

However, as the world slowly returned to a semblance of normalcy, whispers of a new danger emerged. Rumors spread of a shadowy organization, remnants of the New Dawn, plotting their revenge. The agents and the Western economies remained vigilant, knowing that the fight to safeguard humanity was far from over.

In the end, "Viral Vendetta" served as a stark reminder of the lengths some would go to obtain power and the resilience of those who stood against them. It warned of the dangers of unchecked scientific advancements and the need for balance between progress and responsibility.

The world held its breath, ready to face whatever challenges lay ahead, knowing that only through unity and unwavering determination could they ensure the survival of mankind.

Mission: Vindictive Triumph

Ramesh Parwar was a man of few words, but his reputation preceded him. A decorated former special forces operative, he had been chosen to lead a top-secret mission against a Pakistani terrorist organization known as Al-Nuri, responsible for a series of devastating plane hijacks and bomb blasts in India over the past five years. Ramesh Parwar had witnessed firsthand the horrors of their actions and was determined to put an end to their reign of terror.

Set in the bustling city of New Delhi, the story begins with Ramesh Parwar receiving a classified briefing at an undisclosed location. The intelligence reports painted a grim picture of the scale and audacity of Al-Nuri's operations. The group was highly organized and elusive, making it difficult to gather actionable intelligence. As Ramesh reviewed the case files, he felt a mix of determination and a tinge of fear. He knew that this mission would test him in ways he had never imagined.

With a small team of handpicked operatives, Ramesh Parwar began his investigation, starting with the last known locations of Al-Nuri's key members. His team followed leads, interrogated suspects, and worked tirelessly to gather evidence. They soon discovered a pattern—a series of hidden safe houses scattered across the city, acting as operational hubs for the terrorists. Each location was carefully fortified and guarded by a web of informants and trusted allies.

As Ramesh and his team dug deeper, they uncovered a web of deceit and betrayal that reached into the highest echelons of power. It became apparent that Al-Nuri had infiltrated the government, with influential figures turning a blind eye to their activities. The mission took a dangerous turn when Ramesh's team was ambushed during a raid on one of the safe houses. Lives were lost, and Ramesh narrowly escaped with his own.

Refusing to be deterred, Ramesh intensified his efforts. He knew he needed to outthink his adversaries if he had any hope of success. With the help of a trusted hacker, he began unraveling Al-Nuri's communication channels, intercepting coded messages that revealed their plans for a massive attack. Time was running out.

Ramesh Parwar hatched a daring plan to strike at the heart of Al-Nuri's leadership. He enlisted the help of an undercover agent who had infiltrated the organization. Together, they orchestrated a complex ruse, luring Al-Nuri's top commanders into a trap. The stage was set for a final showdown in an abandoned warehouse on the outskirts of New Delhi.

The tension mounted as Ramesh and his team closed in on their targets. They could hear the faint sound of footsteps echoing through the darkened halls. Shadows danced on the walls as the two forces circled each other, each waiting for the perfect moment to strike. The atmosphere was thick with anticipation and the smell of bloodshed.

In a climactic battle, Ramesh Parwar and his team fought with unmatched ferocity. The odds seemed insurmountable, but they pressed on, driven by their mission and a desire for justice. The warehouse became a battleground, filled with gunfire, explosions, and the screams of the wounded. Amidst the chaos, Ramesh confronted the leader of Al-Nuri, a man who personified evil.

Locked in a deadly struggle, Ramesh and his adversary fought with a desperate intensity. Each blow was fueled by years of pain and loss. The outcome of this final confrontation would determine the fate of countless lives. With a final, decisive move, Ramesh Parwar overpowered his enemy and brought him to justice.

The mission was a success. Al-Nuri's leadership was decimated, and their reign of terror came to an end. Ramesh Parwar emerged from the shadows, battered but victorious. He knew, however, that the fight against terrorism was far from over. There would always be new threats, new enemies to face.

As Ramesh Parwar looked out over the city of New Delhi, he felt a mix of relief and determination. He had made a difference, but he knew he couldn't rest on his laurels. The struggle continued, and he was ready to face whatever challenges lay ahead.

Agent 69: Shadows Unleashed

Chapter 1: Agent 69's Assignment

Arthur Cornell Bhattacharya, known as Agent 69 in the clandestine world of assassins, was the most feared and renowned hitman in the industry. He had a reputation for being emotionless, efficient, and ruthless. But deep down, there was a flicker of justice that burned within him.

One fateful night, Agent 69 received an encrypted message, bearing his unique calling card, requesting his services. The message detailed a disturbing truth: an underground sex trafficking empire was operating globally, ensnaring innocent lives in its cruel web. The task was to eliminate every person involved, from the kingpins to the lowest pawns.

Chapter 2: The Advocate

As Agent 69 delved into the heart of the sex trafficking network, he discovered a hidden ally in an unexpected place. Priya Sharma, a passionate and relentless advocate of the Indian Supreme Court, had been fighting against human trafficking for years. Sensing a common purpose, Agent 69 sought her help, knowing that together they could make a difference.

Priya was initially skeptical of Agent 69's motives and methods, but she soon realized his unwavering determination and unmatched skills. The two formed an unlikely alliance, fueled by their shared desire to eradicate the vile trade that destroyed countless lives.

Chapter 3: The Twists Unfold

As Agent 69 and Priya delved deeper into their mission, they faced a series of unexpected twists and turns. They encountered double agents, corrupt officials, and dangerous criminals lurking in the shadows. Each step closer to the truth seemed to invite danger and raise the stakes.

During their perilous journey, Agent 69 and Priya discovered a connection between the sex trafficking ring and powerful individuals in the highest echelons of society. They realized that their mission was not just about eliminating criminals; it was about dismantling a far-reaching network that thrived on wealth and influence.

Chapter 4: Honeymoon in Singapore

Despite the constant danger surrounding them, Agent 69 and Priya managed to find solace in their blossoming relationship. After a particularly grueling mission, they decided to take a break and celebrate their love in Singapore. The city's vibrant energy and romantic ambiance provided the perfect backdrop for their honeymoon.

However, their bliss was short-lived. In a tragic turn of events, Priya was caught in the crossfire of a botched assassination attempt. As she lay lifeless in Agent 69's arms, he vowed to avenge her death and fulfill their shared mission, regardless of the cost.

Chapter 5: Revenge and Redemption

Heartbroken and consumed by vengeance, Agent 69, still unknown by his original name, rallied the support of two formidable agents from the Indian Research and Analysis Wing (RAW): Jack and Jaiswal. The trio embarked on a relentless pursuit of justice, leaving no stone unturned in their search for the masterminds behind Priya's murder.

Together, they faced countless obstacles, including treacherous betrayals, near-death encounters, and the constant threat of discovery. The mission tested their limits physically, mentally, and emotionally, but their unwavering determination fueled their resolve.

Chapter 6: The Final Confrontation

After overcoming extreme hardships and eliminating key players in the sex trafficking network, Agent 69 and his allies finally closed in on the ultimate culprits. As the pieces of the puzzle fell into place, they discovered that one of the kingpins was none other than a high-ranking government official, hidden in plain sight.

In a heart-stopping climax, Agent 69 confronted the corrupt official, exposing his heinous crimes to the world. But victory came at a price. Jack, Agent 69's trusted companion, succumbed to his injuries, sacrificing himself to ensure justice was served.

Chapter 7: A Bittersweet End

As the dust settled and the truth prevailed, Agent 69, now known as Arthur Cornell Bhattacharya, stood alone, gazing at the aftermath of his relentless pursuit. The world was rid of the sex trafficking menace, but he had paid a heavy price for that victory.

Overwhelmed with grief and plagued by the memories of his lost love, Priya, Arthur found no solace in his triumph. The once fearless and determined Agent 69 was now a broken man, haunted by the shadows of his past.

In the final scene, Arthur retreated into the darkness, his tears mingling with the rain. The world may have been saved, but for him, there was no redemption. The story ends on a somber note, a testament to the sacrifices made in the pursuit of justice.

Epilogue: Legacy of Shadows

The legacy of Agent 69, Priya Sharma, and Jack lived on, etched in the annals of justice. Their story became a legend whispered among those who dared to challenge the darkness. The fight against sex trafficking continued, fueled by their sacrifice, reminding the world that heroes could rise even in the most desolate of times.

And so, the tale of Shadows of Vengeance concluded, leaving behind a bittersweet memory of love, loss, and the relentless pursuit of justice in a world plagued by darkness.

Rekindled Love

Once upon a time in the vibrant city of Mumbai, there existed a mischievous yet lovable teenager named Ajit Gupta. With his unruly hair and mischievous grin, Ajit was known for his quick wit and infectious charm. Ajit's best friend, Priyanka Roy, was his perfect foil. Beautiful, intelligent, and with a heart as big as the ocean, Priyanka was the anchor in Ajit's chaotic life.

At their high school, Ajit and Priyanka were inseparable. They would often be seen engaging in playful banter and teasing each other mercilessly. Yet, beneath their pranks and jokes, there was an unbreakable bond of friendship that nobody could penetrate. They supported and loved each other dearly, always there to lend a helping hand or a listening ear.

Their idyllic lives took an unexpected turn when Ajit's father was transferred to the United States for work. The news came as a shock to both Ajit and Priyanka, as they realized their time together was limited. As Ajit bid farewell to his beloved city, Priyanka couldn't hold back her tears. She knew she would miss him terribly, and their relationship came to an abstract and incomplete stop.

Years flew by, and destiny had its own plans in store for Ajit and Priyanka. Priyanka, now a skilled and compassionate doctor, received a prestigious scholarship to pursue her master's degree in the United States. Excitement filled her heart as she embarked on a new chapter of her life.

As fate would have it, on her first day at Stanford University, Priyanka found herself face to face with a familiar figure. It was Ajit, but not the mischievous teenager she once knew. He had transformed into a handsome and charismatic professor, respected by his students and admired by his colleagues.

Their eyes met, and a rush of memories flooded their hearts. Priyanka couldn't contain her joy as she ran towards Ajit, enveloping him in a warm embrace. The years apart melted away, and their lost love regained momentum.

Ajit and Priyanka spent every waking moment together, reliving their cherished memories from high school and creating new ones. Their love blossomed, stronger and deeper than ever before. It was not long before they decided to take their relationship to the next level and walked down the aisle, vowing to be together for eternity.

Their life in the United States was nothing short of a fairytale. Ajit's career continued to soar, and Priyanka's passion for medicine flourished as she became a renowned doctor. Their love radiated in their happy home, where laughter echoed through the hallways.

Time flew by, and Priyanka gave birth to two sons and a daughter. Their children inherited their parents' charm and intelligence, making their little family complete. Ajit and Priyanka nurtured their children with love and provided them with the best possible upbringing.

As they sat on their porch one evening, watching their children play, Ajit wrapped his arm around Priyanka. They reminisced about their teenage years, the mischievous pranks, and the heartfelt conversations that had shaped their love story. They realized that their journey had come full circle, from being teenage best friends to becoming soulmates for life.

With hearts filled with gratitude, Ajit and Priyanka looked into each other's eyes and whispered, "We may have lost our way once, but we found each other again. And this time, our love will last a lifetime."

And so, they lived happily ever after, cherishing every moment, grateful for the love they had found, and grateful for the misfortune that had ultimately brought them back together.

I THANK MY READERS wholeheartedly for reading my short story collection. I promise to cater to a wider variety of moods and audiences, with more twists and turns!! Thanks once again ;)

Don't miss out!

Visit the website below and you can sign up to receive emails whenever Saraswata Bhattacharya publishes a new book. There's no charge and no obligation.

https://books2read.com/r/B-A-MQHZ-EQGLC

BOOKS 2 READ

Connecting independent readers to independent writers.

Also by Saraswata Bhattacharya

Saraswata's Short Stories
Stardust Serenede

Watch for more at https://linktr.ee/Onemanwithamilliondreams.

About the Author

Average Teen from Kolkata, India who aspires, dreams, visualises and aims.

✔ Avid Reader

✔ Student

✓Writer

✔ Poet Novelist

✔ Quotesman

✓Artiste

✔ Singer-Songwriter

✓Director-Producer

✓Guitarist

✓Rapper

✓DJ

✓Stargazer

✔ Romantic-Minded

✔ Philanthropist

✔ Book lover

✔ Nature lover

✔ Pet lover

✔ Radical Philosopher ✓Cyclist

✔ Adventurer

Read more at https://linktr.ee/Onemanwithamilliondreams.

About the Publisher